A Christmas Goodnight

By Nola Buck

Illustrated by
Sarah Jane Wright

 KATHERINE TEGEN BOOKS
An Imprint of HarperCollins Publishers

This book is for Granny Weller.
—N.B.

For my mother, who taught me first, and Lynne, my angel
—S.J.W.

Goodnight to the baby in the hay.
Goodnight to the doves, *coo coo.*

Goodnight to the sleepy mother.
Goodnight to Joseph, too.

Goodnight to the tired donkey.
Goodnight to the calf and lamb.

Goodnight to the smallest sparrow.
Goodnight to the ox and ram.

Goodnight to the angel choir.

Goodnight to the star above.

Goodnight to the Holy Family.

Goodnight to the ones we love.

Goodnight to the weary Wise Men.

Goodnight to their camels tall.

Goodnight to the shepherds and their sheep.

Goodnight, goodnight to them all!

Goodnight to the golden glowing moon.
Goodnight to the frosty air.

Goodnight to the snow that's falling down.
Goodnight to the leaping hare.

Goodnight again, sweet baby.
Goodnight, in your bed in the hay.

Goodnight—God bless
the whole wide world,

for tomorrow is Christmas Day!

Katherine Tegen Books is an imprint of HarperCollins Publishers.

A Christmas Goodnight
Text copyright © 2011 by Laura Godwin
Illustrations copyright © 2011 by Sarah Jane Wright
All rights reserved. Manufactured in China.
Library of Congress Cataloging-in-Publication Data is available.
ISBN 978-0-06-166491-5 (trade bdg.) — ISBN 978-0-06-166492-2 (lib. bdg.)

Typography by Dana Fritts
11 12 13 14 15   SCP   10 9 8 7 6 5 4 3 2 1
❖
First Edition